TADEO TURTLE

You are special,

Blessings,

Janis Cox

Psalm 139:13-14
"You made all the delicate, inner parts of my body
and knit me together in my mother's womb.
Thank you for making me so wonderfully complex!
Your workmanship is marvelous — how well I know it."
(New Living Translation)

WRITTEN AND ILLUSTRATED BY
JANIS COX

TADEO TURTLE

ISBN: 978-1-77069-695-2

Word Alive Press
131 Cordite Road, Winnipeg, MB R3W 1S1
www.wordalivepress.ca

WORD ALIVE PRESS
Just Write!

Library and Archives Canada Cataloguing in Publication

Cox, Janis, 1949-
    Tadeo Turtle / Janis Cox.

ISBN 978-1-77069-695-2

    I. Title.

PS8605.O93545T33 2012   jC813'.6   C2012-904875-5

DEDICATION

*Thanks to my grandchildren,
whom God made and who inspired me
to write this story.*

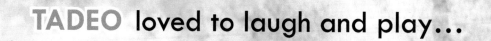

TADEO loved to laugh and play…

...until he met **SAM SQUIRREL** one day.

SAMMY loved to climb the trees,
cross the lawns and jump in leaves.

4

TADEO couldn't run like that
because a shell was on his back.

His carapace* helped him hide
when he stuck his head inside.

* Carapace – A hard outer covering or shell

One day **TADEO** had a dream.
His shell fell off into a stream.
He was free to jump and run.
He climbed trees and had some fun.

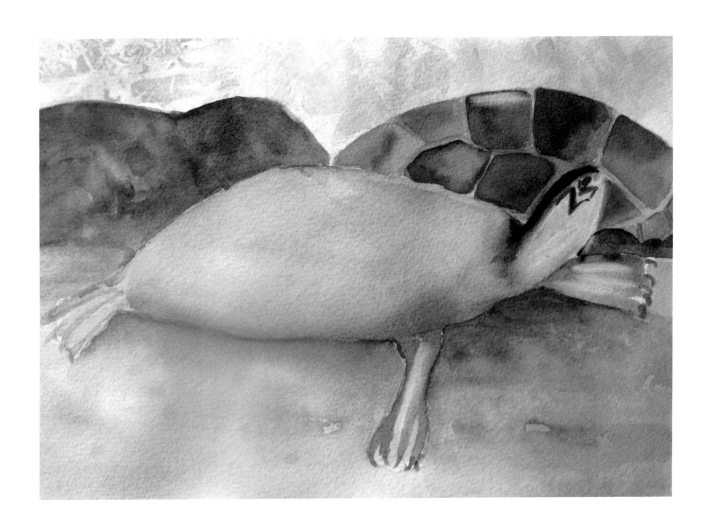

All at once he saw CAT
who thought he was a yummy rat.
The chase was on — he did run.
Now he knew this was not fun.

He ran fast to find his shell
but could not find it very well.
It looked like the river shore
— stones and rocks.
He looked some more.

TADEO hid behind one stone.
He hoped that CAT would go back home.
CAT looked at the riverbed.
"I don't like water," he said.

TAD felt safe behind that stone.
It felt familiar, smelled like home.
"Oh my!" he said. "It is mine."
He plopped it on — just in time.

At that moment TAD awoke.
He knew his shell was not a joke.
God had made him just like that,
not as a squirrel, a cat, or rat.

God had made him perfectly,
not as a fish, a bird, or bee.
With a hard protective shell
he could live his life quite well.

ACTIVITIES

PAPER PLATE TURTLE

Paint a paper plate. Using either craft sticks or construction paper, make 4 legs, 1 head, and 1 tail. Put googly eyes on the head. Decorate the shell with anything you wish. I used scrapbooking paper. Put 5 lines for the toes.

DOUGH TURTLE

Make dough using 1 cup flour, 1/2 cup salt, 1 tbsp. oil, up to 1 cup water. (You may need more if the dough is dry or less if the dough is sticky.) Mix together and knead until rubbery. Take half the dough and make a shell. Cut the other half into 6 pieces. Roll into balls. Make a head and 4 feet. Then divide the last piece in half. Use one half for the tail. Put the other piece aside. Form your turtle using a little water to join the pieces. When finished, line a baking pan with foil. Put the creation on the foil. Use the leftover piece of dough to hold up the head. Bake for 1 hour at 250 degrees Fahrenheit. After cooling, rebake for another hour at the same temperature. Cool again and paint. Be creative.

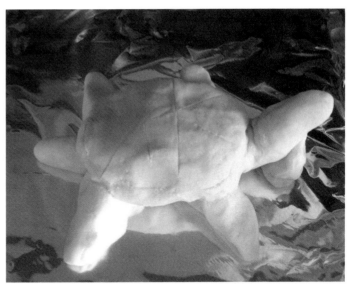

ROCK TURTLE

Find a round flat rock. Paint the shell like a turtle. Use craft sticks to make the feet, head, and tail. Cut one craft stick in half for the head and tail. Paint the craft sticks. Use markers or paint to make details on the shell. Hot-glue the craft sticks to the body.

FELT BOARD

Make a felt board by gluing felt to a piece of cardboard. Cut out pieces of felt to make a turtle, rocks, and water. Use this as a storyboard to recreate the story. Have Tadeo poke his head from behind the rocks as he looks for Cat.

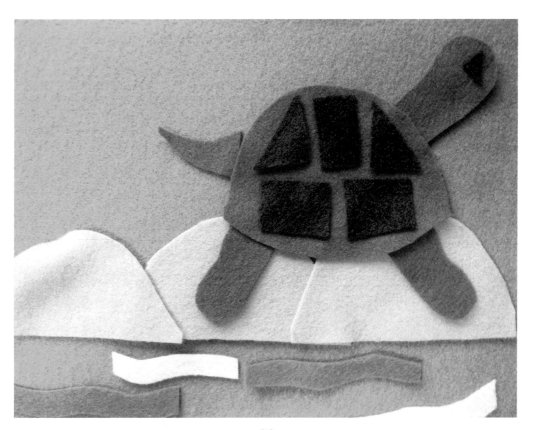

RESEARCH

Research turtles. There are many, many types. God made each one unique.

The largest turtle is the leatherback turtle which can weigh over 900 kg. (about 2000 pounds). Check out:

http://kids.nationalgeographic.com/kids/animals/creaturefeature/leatherback-sea-turtle/

For information on painted turtles check out:

http://www.smm.org/warnernaturecenter/animals/paintedturtle

Many turtles are endangered. Can you find out which ones?
Check out some facts about the Green Turtle:

http://www.konicaminolta.com/kids/endangered_animals/library/sea/green-turtle.html

God made all animals to have some type of defence system from predators. A painted turtle has a shell. Check out other animal defence systems. For example a giraffe has very good eyesight and height so he can have an excellent view of the terrain around him. He has a keen sense of smell and his hearing is very sharp. He can run up to almost 48 kilometres per hour (30 miles per hour). Can you find other examples of animal defence systems?

ABOUT THE AUTHOR

Janis Cox

During retirement, Janis (a retired elementary schoolteacher) has learned to love writing and painting. Janis and her husband have three grown children and enjoy reading and playing with their many grandchildren.

The turtle, Tadeo, is similar to a painted turtle. When Janis painted the turtle, she used her imagination to create Tadeo's colours. The name Tadeo (pronounced TAD-ay-OH) comes from the name Thaddeus which means "heart" or "praise".

She would appreciate hearing from you!
Email: authorjaniscox@gmail.com
Website: www.janiscox.com

CPSIA information can be obtained
at www.ICGtesting.com
Printed in the USA
LVIC091901221012

303892LV00003B